AF606709

SNEAK PEEK
@ SNEAKERS
ADIDAS
adidas
adidas
adidas
Kerrily Sapet

PUBLISHERS

mitchelllane.com

2001 SW 31st Avenue
Hallandale, FL 33009

First Edition, 2021.
Author: Kerrily Sapet
Designer: Ed Morgan
Editor: Sharon F. Doorasamy

Series: Sneak Peek @ Sneakers
Title: Adidas / by Kerrily Sapet

Hallandale, FL : Mitchell Lane Publishers, [2021]

Library bound ISBN: 978-1-68020-642-5
eBook ISBN: 978-1-68020-643-2

PHOTO CREDITS: cover: shutterstock, p. 5 Dutch National Archives public domain, p. 8 Thilo Parg / Wikimedia Commons CC BY-SA 3.0, p. 11 Sueddeutsche Zeitung Photo / Alamy Stock Photo, p. 13 loc.gov, p. 17 Shutterstock.com, p. 18 APimages, pp. 20-21 Shutterstock.com, pp. 22-23 Shutterstock.com, p. 24, Shutterstock.com, p. 25 nasa.gov, p. 27 Mirrorpix/Newscom

CONTENTS

chapter 1

SPEEDY SPIKES

When Wilma Rudolph was four years old, she got sick from polio. The disease weakened her left leg. The doctor said Rudolph would never walk again. She didn't believe him. Rudolph wore a big metal brace on her left leg. She did exercises and practiced walking. By the time Rudolph was nine years old, she no longer needed the brace. And she wasn't just walking, she was running. Rudolph's friends nicknamed her "Skeeter." She was small and fast like a mosquito.

Rudolph became an American track star. In 1960, she competed at the Olympics in Rome, Italy. Even though Rudolph had a sprained ankle, she won three gold medals and broke world records. People called her "the fastest woman on Earth."

After the Olympics, Rudolph was famous. People even stole her shoes as souvenirs. Rudolph wore special lightweight racing shoes with spikes at the toes. The spikes helped her dig in, push off, and speed down the track. Rudolph's shoes were designed by Adolf Dassler, a German shoemaker. He kept the design a secret until the Olympics. Dassler owned the company Adidas. Over the years, thousands of athletes, such as Muhammed Ali and Cristiano Ronaldo, have competed in Adidas shoes.

Skeeter wasn't Wilma Rudolph's only nickname. Her athletic ability and speed earned her three more, "The Black Gazelle," "The Tornado," and "The Black Pearl."

chapter 1

Athletes haven't always had specially designed footwear. The first Olympic athletes, in Greece in 776 BCE, ran barefoot. Shoes were made to protect people's feet from hot sand, snow, rocks, and sticks. Cobblers used leather, fabric, and wood to make shoes. Shoes were often uncomfortable, stiff, and noisy.

People began experimenting with other materials. They used a thick fabric called canvas and tried making soles with rubber from trees in South America. The rubber melted into sticky ooze in hot weather. It got hard and cracked in cold weather. In 1839, Charles Goodyear, an inventor, mixed hot rubber with chemicals to create a strong, flexible rubber. He called it **vulcanized rubber**. He named it after Vulcan, the Roman god of fire.

TENNIES, TRAINERS, AND TAKKIES

People around the world call sneakers by different names. In the eastern United States, they're "sneakers." In the Midwest, they're "tennis shoes." Sneakers are also known as "gym shoes," "kicks," "daps," "gutties," and "plimsolls" because early rubber-soled shoes had a stripe like a line called a "plimsoll" on a boat. Whatever the name, they're the most popular shoes on Earth.

chapter 1

FAST FACT:

In 1991, hikers discovered a 5,300-year-old ice mummy. The Iceman wore shoes made of tough bearskin, braided tree bark, and dried grass.

This reconstruction of Ötzi the Iceman, Europe's oldest mummy, is on display in a museum in Italy.

Shoes with rubber soles became popular. People called them "sneakers." The soles were so quiet people could sneak up on each other. Today, everyone from babies to grandparents wears sneakers. In 2018, people worldwide spent $64 billion on sneakers. Many of those sneakers were made by Adidas.

chapter 2

ENEMY BROTHERS

Adolf Dassler, the founder of Adidas, was born in 1900 in Herzogenaurach, Germany. His family called him "Adi." Adi's father, Christoph, worked in a shoe factory. His mother, Pauline, ran a small laundry business. Adi and his older brother, Rudolf, delivered the clean laundry to her customers. When Adi was older, he trained to become a baker. But he was more interested in shoemaking.

After World War I, Adi's family needed money. He decided to try making and selling shoes. Adi scavenged the nearby forest for helmets, leather bags, and silk parachutes left behind by soldiers. He used the bits and pieces to make shoes.

"I grew up in a working class family. We weren't poor, but we were awful close." Adolf "Adi" Dassler (1900–1978)

chapter 2

In 1924, Adi and Rudolf founded the Dassler Brothers Shoe Factory. They used their mother's laundry room as a workshop. Sometimes the town's electricity didn't work. Adi rigged up a bicycle that they could pedal to power their equipment.

Adi loved sports. He believed that if athletes had better shoes they could run faster, jump higher, and win more. Adi studied old athletic shoes and tinkered in his workshop. He experimented with unusual materials, such as shark skin and kangaroo leather, to make lightweight, strong shoes. Adi's **innovative** racing shoes looked like ballet slippers with long, toothy metal spikes.

In 1936, Adi and Rudolf packed a suitcase with their spiked shoes. They drove to Berlin, Germany, for the Olympics. The Dasslers convinced athletes, including American track and field star Jesse Owens, to wear their spiked shoes. When Owens won four gold medals, the Dassler Brothers Shoe Factory became famous. Within two years, they were making 1,000 shoes a day.

Sprinter Jesse Owens felt snubbed by President Franklin D. Roosevelt after his historic wins in 1936. However, in 1976 President Gerard R. Ford awarded him the Presidential Medal of Freedom, the nation's highest civilian honor.

chapter 2

During World War II, Adi ran the factory. They made boots for soldiers. Rudolf served as a soldier in the German army. The brothers had different personalities and beliefs. They argued and became enemies. In 1948, they divided their factory. Rudolf moved across the river and started his own company. Adi named his company "Adidas," for his first and last initials. Rudolf did the same. Later, Rudolf changed his company's name from "Ruda" to "Puma."

The argument between the brothers split the town. Adults and children formed Adidas and Puma gangs. Bakers loyal to Adidas wouldn't sell bread to people wearing Puma sneakers. It became known as the "town of the bent necks" because people always looked down at each other's sneakers.

Adi and Rudolf never forgave each other. Although they are buried in the same cemetery, their graves are as far apart as possible. Adidas and Puma continue to compete with each other today, each trying to sell the most shoes.

Adi Dassler wanted everyone to recognize Adidas sneakers. He needed a logo. For years, Dassler had added two leather strips to the sides of shoes to strengthen them. In 1952, he bought a black three-stripe logo from a company called Karhu. Dassler paid approximately $1,000.00. In 2018, Adidas sold 409 million pairs of sneakers. That's a lot of stripes!

chapter 3

SNEAKERS EVERYWHERE

For years, only athletes wore sneakers. Then people realized sneakers were less expensive than leather shoes. They also were more comfortable because they had bouncy rubber soles. Today, everyone from babies taking their first steps to astronauts on the International Space Station wears sneakers. People don't just wear sneakers when they play sports. They also wear them to show their personal style.

At first, sneakers were just black and white. Now, they are made in a rainbow of colors. Sneakers come in all shapes and sizes. There are sneakers for size 1 baby feet, size 22 basketball player feet, and all sizes in between. Sneakers come in low-tops, high-tops, and even dressy high heels. They lace, Velcro, zip, bungee, and even just slip on.

Companies, such as Adidas, sell sneakers for every sport. Adidas even makes sneakers for boxers, mountain climbers, and gymnasts. Sneaker companies compete to design sneakers with the latest technology and in the most popular styles. They also make sportswear. Adidas is the second-biggest sneaker company in the world. Only Nike sells more sneakers.

To make their shoes even more popular, companies **sponsor** athletes. They pay sports stars to wear and advertise their sneakers. Adidas has sponsored athletes such as Stan Smith, David Beckham, and Alvin Kamara. Sneaker companies also work with actors, musicians, and celebrities to create sneakers in the hottest styles. Adidas has partnered with Beyoncé, Katy Perry, and Kanye West.

New Orleans Saints running back Alvin Kamara signed a multiyear contract with Adidas.

Sneakers are a big business. In 2018, Adidas sold approximately $24 billion in sneakers and sportswear. Experts predict by 2025, people worldwide will spend $95 billion a year on sneakers. Most sneakers are made in Korea and China. Sneakers are packed on planes, trains, and ships, and delivered around the world. Adidas's robotic Speedfactories crank out 1 million pairs of shoes a year. There are approximately 15 billion feet in the world and many of them are wearing Adidas striped sneakers.

FAST FACT:

Sailors on submarines wear sneakers because they are quieter than heavy, clunky work boots and safer for climbing steep, narrow ladders.

chapter 4

FUTURISTIC KICKS

To improve his designs, Adi Dassler talked to athletes. He took notes and observed feet. He even met with doctors to design shoes for injured athletes. Dassler thought about the surfaces on which athletes compete. Tracks made of rubbery materials are rough when dry and slippery when wet. Soccer fields are slick, muddy messes in the rain. Dassler added spikes and other features depending on the sport.

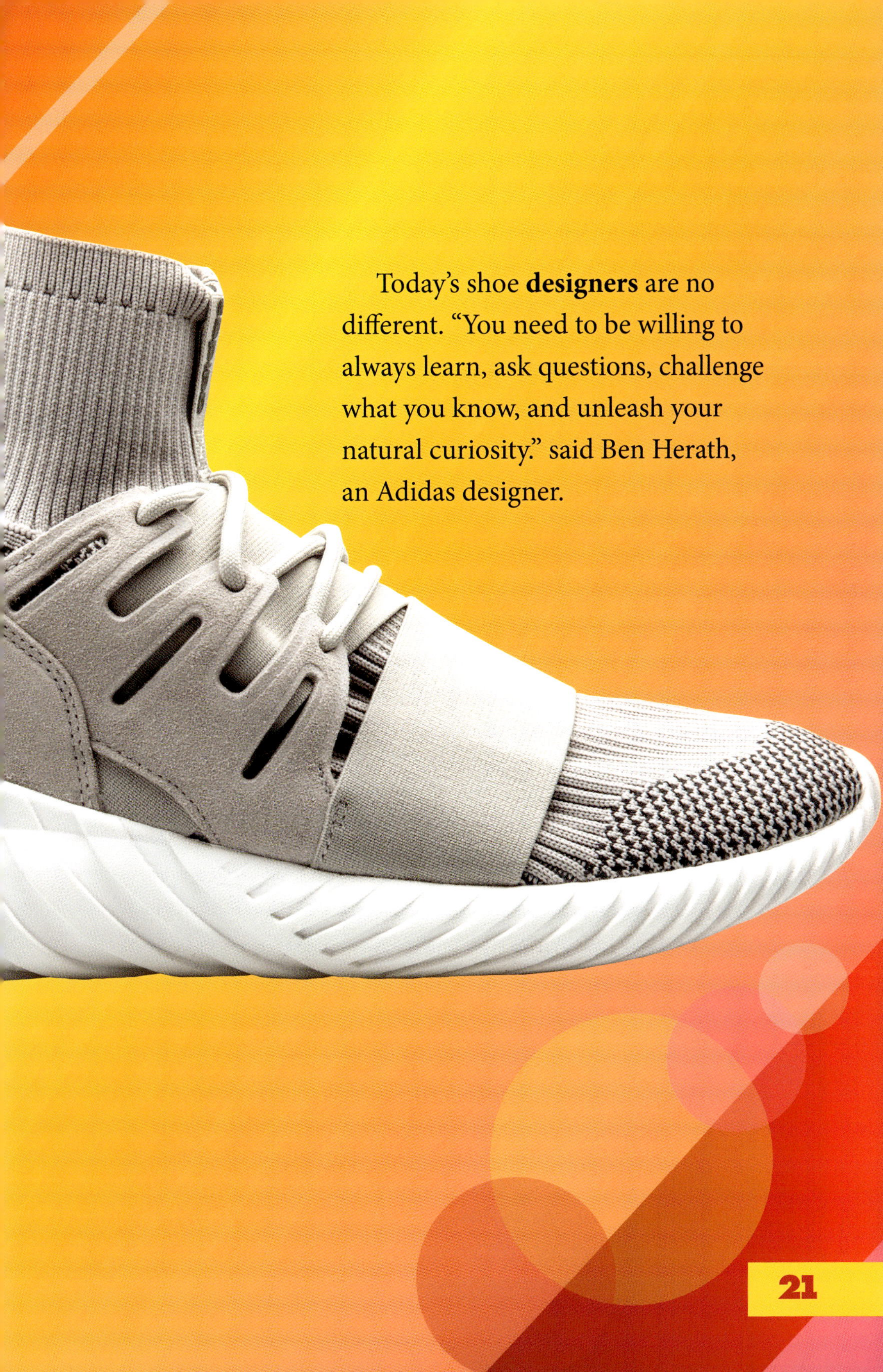

Today's shoe **designers** are no different. "You need to be willing to always learn, ask questions, challenge what you know, and unleash your natural curiosity." said Ben Herath, an Adidas designer.

Designers, developers, and artists team up to create a new sneaker. They start with a sketch. They think about weight, materials, cushioning, style, and cost. Sneakers are made from leather, fabric, rubber, plastic, and **synthetics**. Synthetics are combinations of man-made materials. Designers use gels, foams, and air bubbles to add cushioning. They also test new materials. Adidas partnered with Continental Tire to create a shoe from rubber developed for motorcycle tires for use in the rain. Their first shoe had so much grip it stuck to walls.

Designers often get their ideas from the world around them. Adidas uses a strong, lightweight fabric made from fake spiderweb silk grown in a laboratory. Adidas's XENO shoes were inspired by the Xenopeltis snake from Asia. The snake's scales change color in the light. Adidas's designers created a snakeskin-like fabric that looks black but erupts in shimmering colors under bright lights.

Designers are testing new technologies, such as 3D printing. They feed plastic into 3D printers to print **prototypes** of new shoes. They also use 3D printing to custom design shoes for customers. Someday people may be able to print their own shoes at home in a few hours.

Companies are working to make environmentally friendly sneakers. Adidas uses plastic scooped from the ocean to make its Futurecraft.Loop sneaker. "It's possible to turn ocean plastic into something cool," said Cyrill Gutsch, an environmentalist. Adidas melts the used sneakers to create plastic to make more sneakers. Other companies are using plastic bags, tires, and fishing nets to make sneakers.

Today's sneakers are packed with technology. Some have tiny computers that identify the person wearing them. Others connect to apps to display pictures, lace themselves, and heat your feet. Sneakers in the future may be able to do even more.

FROM SPACESUITS TO SNEAKERS

Technology developed by NASA, the National Aeronautics and Space Administration, has changed life on Earth. NASA scientists developed a process called "blow rubber molding" to create lightweight, strong space helmets. Today, shoe companies use blow rubber molding to make sneakers with soles that can be filled with shock-absorbing materials. Millions of sneaker wearers walk in astronaut-inspired shoes every day.

chapter 5

SPORTS & STYLE

Look at someone's feet and chances are that you'll see sneakers. They are everywhere. We see them on everyone from Olympians to grandmothers doing aerobics. The **slogans** used to advertise sneakers, such as Adidas's "Impossible is Nothing" and Nike's "Just Do It," inspire people to run faster, jump higher, and push themselves.

Today's sneakers are a combination of fitness and fashion. Some people choose sneakers for sports. Others pick sneakers because they like the fit or feel. Some people want the sneakers their favorite sports star or celebrity wears.

Tens of thousands of Run-D.M.C. fans lifted their Adidas sneakers into the air at a 1986 New York City performance by the rap group.

In the 1980s, sneakers became more than just shoes. Wearing a pair of Nike "Air Jordans" showed that kids could grow up to be a star basketball player like Michael Jordan. Brands of sneakers appeared in movies and songs. Members of the hip-hop band Run-D.M.C. sang a song called "My Adidas." "In our minds, fresh sneakers were better than the finest jewelry and the finest cars," said Darryl McDaniels of Run-D.M.C.

Resell values for the Adidas 350 Boost V2 "Beluga," pictured above, range from $691 to $1,200.

Companies, such as Adidas, work with athletes and celebrities to produce new designs. In 2019, Adidas sold $1.9 billion in Yeezy Boost sneakers designed by Kanye West. Adidas partners with movie studios and young designers. They have made Marvel superhero, Star Wars, and pepperoni pizza-themed shoes. Popular sneakers, such as Yeezys, sell out in minutes. People camp out in front of stores to be the first to buy them.

Shoe collectors, nicknamed "sneakerheads," buy sneakers to wear, to add to their collections, or to sell. Rare sneakers sell for thousands of dollars. Jordy Geller holds a world record for owning the most pairs of sneakers. "Shoes stand for stories, and history, and innovation, and what athletes did in those shoes," Geller says.

Today's sneaker designs have been inspired by astronauts, spiders, and snakes. Sneakers made by Adidas are everywhere. Athletes, celebrities, and kids lace up their sneakers when they compete, run down the street, and show their style.

SNEAKER SPEAK

At Sneaker Con, a traveling convention, sneakerheads meet to buy, sell, and swap sneakers. They even have their own sneaker language. A pair of new shoes is called "deadstock." The combination of colors and symbols on a sneaker is a "colorway." An older, worn sneaker is a "beater." The shoe someone wants more than any other pair is a "grail."

GLOSSARY

designer
A person who creates original products

innovative
New and different

logo
A picture or symbol

prototype
The first design or model

slogan
A saying used to advertise an item

sponsor
A company that pays someone to advertise or wear their product

synthetics
Man-made materials

vulcanized rubber
Rubber mixed with chemicals to become stronger

TIMELINE

1924 Rudolf and Adolf Dassler open the Dassler Brothers Shoe Factory.

1948 The brothers split their company into Adidas and Puma.

1949 The three-stripe logo is incorporated.

1956 Olympic athletes win 72 medals in Adidas sneakers.

1960 At the Rome Olympics, 75% of all track and field athletes wore Adidas shoes including Wilma Rudolph.

1978 Adi Dassler dies.

1986 Run-DMC partnership with Adidas is the very first endorsement deal in Rap history.

1997 Adidas begins sponsoring David Beckham.

2015 Adidas partners with Kanye West.

2019 Adidas begins working with Beyoncé.

FURTHER READING

Cole, Jason. *Golden Kicks: The Shoes that Changed Sport*. New York, NY: Bloomsbury Sport, 2016.

Keyser, Amber J. *Sneaker Century: A History of Athletic Shoes*. Minneapolis, MN: Twenty-First Century Books, 2015.

Le Maux, Mathieu. *1000 Sneakers: A Guide to the World's Greatest Kicks, from Sport to Street*. New York, NY: Rizzoli Publications, 2016.

Morganelli, Adriana. *Wilma Rudolph: Track and Field Champion*. Ontario, Canada: Crabtree Publishing Company, 2016.

Nelson, Robin. *From Leather to Basketball Shoes*. Minneapolis, MN: Lerner Publishing Group, 2014.

INDEX

ABOUT THE AUTHOR

Kerrily Sapet has written more than 30 books for children. Sneakers are her go-to shoes for work, home, and outdoor activities. While researching this book, she enjoyed learning about Adidas's recyclable shoes and plans to try them out for her next pair of running shoes.